1

Cottage Dreams

A Moriston House Mystery

Jennifer A. Girardin

The Moriston House Mystery Series
By Jennifer A. Girardin

The Cottage Crimes Collection

Classic British Mysteries

Cottage Dreams

Cottage Dreams

A Cottage Crimes Mystery

Jennifer Anne Girardin

Author of Moriston House British Mysteries and Classical Pianist

Notes from the Crime

Murder never sleeps as Lord Hugo Anstead and the Mayfair Detective Agency investigate the mysterious death of housekeeper Louise Greene at idyllic Haldon Cottage . . . where nothing is quite what it seems. Everyone at Haldon Cottage had a reason to commit the crime, including the famous retired violinist, Rose Pendlebury, her romance scammer nephew, Alan, and his desperate and clingy girlfriend, Anna Henderson. When Lord Hugo and the village sleuths go undercover at the elegant country estate, they unravel a trail of false clues and danger as they race to solve the case before the murderer strikes again. Happy sleuthing from Moriston House books!

Chapter One

"Do you believe in ghosts?" Elizabeth Branell-Markson whispered, shivering as she consulted the inexplicable file from their new client, Rose Pendlebury.

"I'm a practical person, my dear," Rose replied prosaically, rubbing a restless hand over her string of heirloom pearls. "I've never believed in spooks or haunted houses . . . until I moved into Haldon Cottage."

Even now she could hardly say the name—or believe that she was consulting England's most renowned private detective agency.

Elizabeth poured her another cup of tea and awaited a glorious outcome. There was something infinitely soothing in a cozy cup of tea. It invited confidence and trust—and had served many hopeless investigations. The national beverage never let you down. Her voice was encouraging and persuasive.

"We must know everything if we are to help you."

The Mayfair Detective Agency certainly lived up to its reputation. Moriston House, Lord Hugo Anstead's elegant country estate in the English countryside, provided an ideal background for crime. Set near the glorious village of Halfereton, where wandering lanes and cozy cottages slept among sweetly planted gardens and rolling green pastures, life was certainly quiet . . . until now.

Elizabeth Branell-Markson lingered over her

cup of tea and assembled the facts of the case with an ease that betrayed her years. As the youngest member of their unique detective agency, she seldom took anything at face value. She was a tall and vibrant eleven-year-old, with wavy ginger hair, keen amber eyes, and the power of a steam engine. She was first in her class, impossibly inquisitive, and dangerously intelligent. In her spare time, she wrote a celebrated crime column for the local newspaper, the *Halfereton Times,* under the nom de plume of Miranda Jones. She read poetry with a compulsion that flabbergasted her teacher, quoted Shakespeare and Jane Austen with such practiced delicacy as to astonish the natives, and was dangerously fluent in politics, news, and economics. She lived for crime and was well versed in forensic science, and she kept a meticulous journal of the cases that graced their distinguished agency. Her father, William, a drowsy and simple country librarian, was blissfully ignorant of his daughter's involvement in solving crimes.

"When did you first notice that something was wrong at Haldon Cottage?" Elizabeth asked gently.

Rose Pendlebury shifted uneasily in her chair and recalled the sensational events that had brought her name to the headlines of crime. She was a tall and plump woman of fifty-nine, with dreamy blue eyes, wild ashy hair, and restless hands. In an attempt to gain the approval of the locals, she wore a conventional tweed skirt, a wooly cashmere cardigan, and sensible Wellies. She was a renowned musician and teacher, and played the violin, flute, and piano. Her arrival in the village of Halfereton had been much anticipated, and her charity concert last week had received critical praise in the local newspaper. In truth, she was relieved to take a break from relentless tours and stressful concerts, petty disputes, ridiculous jealousies, and endless critics. The English countryside had brought her peace of mind . . . and a haunted house.

Rose Pendlebury finished her fragrant cup of tea and took a deep breath. She felt exactly as she did before an opening night performance: anxious, lost, and hopelessly restless. Once the music started everything went back to normal and the world was once again at peace, but those fragile moments before the curtain rose were distinctly uncomfortable and open to the gravest sensations. There were times when she wondered how she ever could perform. Her confidence dangled upon a very tight rope, and her hands trembled in waves of uncertainty. Shyness was a silent disease and had haunted her for as long as she could remember. It was one of her best-kept secrets—and private agonies. To the public, she appeared calm, composed, and perfectly at ease, but inside she lived in a world of complete doubt and endless insecurity.

She placed her cup and saucer on the table in a blend of hope and fear. Her voice was deep and bell-like, and sounded strangely unfamiliar.

"Everything started at teatime."

Elizabeth understood perfectly and gave her an approving glance.

"I was playing a little piece by Mozart when I heard something odd coming from the garden."

"Mozart often has an effect on people," Elizabeth sighed, recalling Rose's performance at the village theatre last week. She had never thought that music could be so beautifully ethereal . . . or that she would be consulting Miss Pendlebury at Moriston House.

"I think our client has more to say, dear," Jane Holden added, and poured her another cup of tea. As the village's premier busybody, she understood the value of discretion. She was a tall and industrious widow, with wispy bobbed hair, penetrating green eyes, and an uncompromising manner. Her aging bachelor son, Neil, was the hardnosed editor of the *Halfereton Times*, and Jane graced the gossip column as the impeccable Miss Manners. Beneath her ladylike demeanor and dainty cardigan twinset, she had solved some of the village's most notorious crimes.

"I saw a figure in the garden by the front gate," Rose trembled, feeling increasingly unwell. "I couldn't see who it was. The person was tall and wore black clothing and was hooded, but they dropped a note before they disappeared."

She passed it to Jane Holden, who was an expert in the fine tradition of dangerous correspondence in the English countryside. Jane adjusted her glasses and examined the note. It was a shabby and amateur attempt, typewritten—who still used a typewriter in 2023? Some people obviously didn't know the first thing about crime.

Leave Haldon Cottage before it's too late . . . or you'll suffer the same fate as Emma Haldon.

"Can you tell us anything else about the intruder in your garden?" Jane asked suspiciously.

"Nothing at all," Rose shivered. "But it was at that moment when I heard a cry coming from the attic. It sounded like the voice of a women—I know it's crazy. I've never believed in ghosts, but since then, there have been several inexplicable incidents at the cottage. I have heard strange footsteps on the stairs and seen shadows creep along the passage. Crockery has shattered in the dead of night."

"Old houses have their little secrets," Jane replied prosaically. She had often thought that every ghost story had started somewhere in the English countryside, but something in the manner of their client gave her pause to consider.

"I know what you're thinking." Rose sighed breathlessly. "But there is something you don't know. My housekeeper, Louise Greene, was attacked last night."

"Did she see anything before she was pushed down the stairs?"

"How did you know she was pushed down

the stairs?"

"We are in England, dear."

"It all happened so quickly."

Jane flipped through her catalogue of crime and paused before a newspaper clipping of Emma Haldon's sudden and inexplicable death. Haldon Cottage had been her family's home for generations. Her sudden death had never been explained.

Emma Haldon had been a close friend and neighbor, and her loss had taken Jane by complete surprise. So many questions lingered in the back of her mind, and the police were in no hurry to answer any of them. She smiled at Lord Hugo Anstead's plummy report, which had made waves throughout the village. He wrote a scandalous column under the pen name of Harold Trent, and he was a ruthless and versatile partner in crime.

*** The Halfereton Times ***

Haldon Cottage Mystery

By H. R. Trent, Local Correspondent.

Tragedy struck at Haldon Cottage after retired local historian Emma Haldon died unexpectedly. Several witnesses observed her walking near the village green with her Collie shortly before she disappeared. Traces of cyanide were found in the victim's evening cup of tea, and an ongoing police investigation has ruled out the possibility of suicide. Private services will be held Saturday at St. Andrew's Church . . .

It had been over a year and the crime had remained unsolved. Jane hated injustice, loose ends, and unsolved crimes. Could there be a connection to the recent events at Haldon Cottage? It seemed impossible, and yet stranger things had occurred . . .

and they had a wondrous tendency of happening in the English countryside.

"It seems to be getting worse," Rose added with a musical sigh.

"Worse?" Jane asked patiently. She had met many reluctant clients in her career as a village criminologist, and she was content to let the situation ripen at its own pace.

"At first, I thought it was all a joke or a simple misunderstanding, but after Louise was attacked last night, I had to do something."

Jane glanced over her notes with a shrewd eye and came to the heart of the matter.

"What are you holding back?"

"The police were very kind and generous in their investigation, but . . ."

Jane could not imagine Inspector James

.

Meriden being kind or generous. He was a slow and dreary middle-aged man with a very fat head and a complete lack of imagination . . . but he wasn't born yesterday.

"I didn't tell them about what was found at the site of Louise's accident. It seemed too trivial and Louise hates publicity. She was terribly disoriented and shaken—the doctor was quite amazed that she had suffered no serious injuries—but I found an old photo at the foot of the stairs. *It's Emma Haldon and her dog, Haydn.*"

"Are you quite certain that it wasn't there before?" Jane asked, examining the faded photo.

"Everything happened so quickly," Rose sighed. "I didn't think the police would be interested in a village ghost story."

She glanced around the elegant living room

at Moriston House and felt an uncanny sense of calm. It was one of the finest houses in England, and was renowned for its beautiful gardens and historical significance. It had been featured in every decorating and gardening magazine in England, and Lord Hugo Anstead and his wife, Lady Rosalin, were a gracious and generous young couple who had devoted their lives to solving local crimes.

Rose glanced out the towering windows, observing a young man riding a strong chestnut horse. The man was tall, dark, and dangerously handsome, and his coat flew behind him as the horse galloped towards the house. It reminded her of a scene from one of Jane Austen's novels. Perhaps Mr. Darcy had come to pay his respects.

"Is that Lord Hugo Anstead?" she asked breathlessly. She squinted and tried to make out the figure with more accuracy but came up blank. Her glasses had a regrettable tendency of disappearing without a trace and then turned up again when didn't need them.

Jane politely suited her response to the occasion. As a celebrated private detective, Lord Hugo Anstead's aliases were one of England's best-kept secrets. He was currently seeking to gain credit for the case by pretending to be Miss Pendlebury's music assistant. Under the alias of Harold Trent, he was a budding musician and part-time columnist for the local newspaper. It would do the investigation no credit if Rose Pendlebury became acquainted with the truth too soon.

"No, dear," Jane smiled convincingly. "That is Lord Hugo's cousin, Harold Trent. He also writes for the newspaper—I believe he's going to assist you."

They watched as the horse was taken to one of the outbuildings. Jane waited patiently, uncertain what to do next. She was about to pour everyone another cup of tea when the terrace doors burst open and the master of the house tumbled into the room.

"Has something happened in the village, Mr. Trent?" Jane asked innocently.

Lord Hugo Anstead took a deep breath and made a gentle bow in the direction of Rose Pendlebury, who felt an unpleasant chill creep down the back of her neck.

"I'm very sorry to inform you that Louise Greene was found dead in the garden at Haldon Cottage."

Chapter Two

"Do the police have any suspects in the case?" Penny Martin asked, cutting an enormous slice of Mrs. Grant's famous chocolate cake. Dinner at Moriston House was always a treat, and Maggie Grant was one of the village's most versatile cooks. She had been the housekeeper at Moriston House since time began, and she was a moody and meticulous middle-aged woman, with wiry grey hair, a generous figure, and a very sharp tongue. She wasn't always pleasant, but she certainly knew how to cook.

"No," Jane Holden replied, and poured her

another cup of coffee.

Penny Martin sighed indulgently and stirred her coffee, feeling that something must be done . . . and it must be done now. She disliked perfect alibis, loose ends, and cold cases. After an exhausting lifetime spent as a glamorous socialite in London, she had come to the countryside to immerse herself in the quiet life. Little could she have known what she was in for! Murder, mayhem, and tea in the afternoon were just a few of life's little treats in the sleepy village of Halfereton. Her husband, Neville, a retired solicitor without an ounce of adventure, slept quietly in the background, drowning himself in pointless rounds of golf and endless club gossip. But Penny Martin had other plans. She was a tall and commanding middle-aged woman with unpredictable auburn hair, dreamy blue eyes, and a robust figure. She wore an ivory cashmere cardigan, an itchy tweed skirt, and bright yellow garden clogs. People invariably asked you to see the garden, and Penny Martin was certainly prepared for anything.

"They say the case will never be solved."

She let the words settle into nothing . . . hoping that something useful might drop in unexpectedly.

"I wouldn't say that, my dear," Jane replied, consulting her notes. "Haldon Cottage has a reputation for dark mysteries and unsolved crimes, but I'm sure something will turn up when you serve breakfast tomorrow morning."

"Why would I be serving breakfast tomorrow morning at Haldon Cottage?" Penny asked, feeling increasingly unwell. Jane's little ideas often involved undercover work, and Penny Martin had a severe dislike for domestic work.

"Rose Pendlebury desperately needs a new housekeeper," Jane replied easily. "I promised to find her a suitable replacement, and you are ideally qualified for the post."

"But . . ."

"Don't worry, my dear. My son, Neil will be on hand sniffing around for clues in the guise of a beginning music student, and Lord Hugo will also be there under Miss Pendlebury's musical wing. His alibi is perfectly genuine, except that Miss Pendlebury is under the impression that he is Harold Trent. Undercover work is such fun, don't you think?"

For once in her life, Penny Martin did not agree. Undercover work was slow, tedious, and at time, dangerous. She could think of better things to do than serving breakfast, cleaning dishes, folding laundry, and mopping floors at Haldon Cottage.

"We're relying on you, dear."

Jane's bell-like voice was engaging, persuasive, and difficult to brush off.

"I knew you wouldn't let us down. But you must be careful."

"I don't think I'll meet any handsome murderers while I'm doing the washing up," Penny sighed, looking down at her perfectly manicured nails. Detective work wasn't always pretty . . . but it was certainly interesting.

"If there is a connection to the death of Emma Haldon, then you must take every possible precaution."

In the same way that Jane would pass the salt or pepper, she placed a revolver beside Mrs. Martin's fine linen napkin. Jane's little ideas often had a way of leaving you breathless . . . and turning out to be completely right. During such delicate moments it was fortunate that Elizabeth Branell-Markson was busy at home studying for her upcoming English exam.

"But I don't know anything about guns."

"That's quite all right, my dear," Jane replied. "We're not asking you to use it."

"I'm delighted to hear it."

"But there is just one thing that doesn't make any sense," Jane added wistfully.

"What's that?"

Jane sighed and shuffled through her notes again, leaving Penny Martin's head whirling.

"Of course it may be a coincidence or it may have nothing to do with the crime, but we must find out what's behind it all."

Penny delicately turned the lethal weapon over and found nothing unusual. It was the first time she had ever seen a gun, let alone touched one. It felt cold, hard, and . . . uncomfortably dangerous.

"Find out what?"

"I'm sorry, my dear," Jane replied, coming back to herself. "As you probably know, the police made a thorough investigation of Haldon Cottage after the recent crime."

"And?"

"They found nothing."

Penny Martin pictured the large and bumbling Inspector James Meriden . . . and his smug attitude towards private detectives.

"I'm not surprised."

"As you know, neither Emma Haldon nor

Louise Greene died as the result of gunshot wounds. The police investigated both scenes and found nothing. Rose Pendlebury does not strike me as the type of person to fiddle with guns, let alone keep one as her bedside companion. In fact, she was horrified at the merest mention of guns when I spoke to her privately. One can learn so much in the garden. She has a patch of dead grass that quite saved the day. I told her what to do about it and Lord Hugo joined us unexpectedly. He is quite knowledgeable about firearms and noticed it at once."

"Noticed what at once?" Penny asked breathlessly.

"That gun was found in the garden at Haldon Cottage. Rose Pendlebury was working in the garden all morning. It struck me as odd that she didn't notice it earlier. I saw it at once, and I'm practically blind."

"So you think that Rose Pendlebury was lying?" Penny asked, shivering at the thought of it all.

"And who is she trying to protect?"

Chapter Three

"Count me out," Neil Holden grumbled, and turned over in his bed. As the editor-in-chief of the local newspaper, the *Halfereton Times*, he hated early mornings, cold coffee, and the daily crossword.

"Everyone is relying on you, dear."

His mother's voice always reminded him of one of those birds that never stop chirping. There were too many damned birds in the English countryside, and the sheer happiness of it all made him sick. He was a disheveled and angry man, strangely attractive and utterly contemptible. He should have moved out years ago, but at the age of forty-three, it seemed unlikely that he was going anywhere at all. Once upon a time, he had his heart set on marrying the village's brightest young woman, but Joan Haldon had ditched him in the last minute in favor of a torrid affair with his best friend. Since then, he had closed his heart off from the world and buried himself in his work, sorting through petty village news and hopeless local gossip. His life was basic, empty, and uncomplicated . . . until now.

"You promised to assist us with the investigation at Haldon Cottage," Jane added, and threw open the window, letting in a breath of fresh country air. Outside, the birds were singing, and the garden bloomed in a lush and ever-changing natural display. Somewhere in the lonely attic room at Jane's idyllic home, Rosewood Cottage, there lived a foolish aging bachelor who had closed himself off from the world. Jane was determined to see justice—and solve the case.

"I don't see why I should be bothered about another murder in the village," he grunted, and grabbed a cigarette from his nightstand.

"We must do what everything we can to find out who murdered Louise Greene," Jane replied pleasantly. "And we must discover if there is a connection to the death of Emma Haldon."

Even now, the merest mention of the name Haldon made him feel unwell. Joan Haldon was Emma's daughter, and their breakup had felt like the end of the world. She had gone off with another man—probably several more since—and he closed that brief chapter without a trace of remorse. But he couldn't help feeling that some things have a strange way of happening for the worst.

"I'm sorry if the case revives bad memories," Jane sighed, picturing how different their lives might have been. She dreamed wistfully of rosy-cheeked grandchildren and cheery Christmas dinners by the fire. Her son had given up on love, but she wasn't going to give up on him. And the sound of their housekeeper's footsteps in the hall brought a sense of urgency to a desperate situation.

"Quick, dear," Jane whispered, and tossed his cigarette out the window. Their unpredictable housekeeper, Hetty Belford, had taken a shine to the unworthy bachelor . . . and she loathed smoking.

"I don't care who sees me smoking," Neil retorted, and lit another cigarette. "I pay endless bills and work like a slave in this shabby country fixer. I waste my life providing the readers of England with well-soaked lies, and I cook a decent Sunday dinner.

I won't stand for it any longer."

Jane brushed a tender hand through his unruly hair and spoke in the same voice she had used when he was three years old.

"We're relying on you, dear."

"Good morning, Neil," Hetty beamed, and brought in a gleaming silver tray. She placed it on his bedside table and kissed him lightly on the cheek, causing him to turn green. The last thing in the world he wanted was cold coffee . . . and a warm kiss from their optimistic housekeeper.

She smiled bewitchingly at him, admiring his windswept hair, muscular shoulders, and strong hands. The merest glimpse of his striped pajamas made her heart flutter. She liked men with strong hands, and blushed at the thought of a cozy night in the lonely attic room at Rosewood Cottage.

"Lord Hugo will be arriving shortly, but if there is anything you need . . ."

"Nothing at all," the editor gulped, ready to jump out the window. "Why the hell would Lord Hugo Anstead come here?"

"Didn't you know?" Hetty blushed, and poured him a steaming cup of coffee. She bent over and whispered some naughty sweet nothings in his ear. He nearly fainted. Perhaps this wasn't going to be as unpleasant as he imagined. "Everyone in the village is talking about it. The murder at Haldon Cottage is still unsolved, and we're relying on you to find out who murdered Louise Greene."

Her sincerity touched him in a strange way— and her coffee was damned good. The sound of the doorbell signaled the end of this battle and a victory for the home team.

"Your first lesson should go smoothly."

"What lesson?" he asked, feeling increasingly unwell. His mother's endless harebrained schemes often left him speechless.

"Miss Pendlebury has agreed to give you music lessons," Hetty replied graciously. "It's quite an honor for us all. And it will be so very pleasant to hear you playing in the evenings. Music is so romantic, sir, and I'm sure you'll play with great passion."

Hetty's ample breast heaved luxuriously as she dreamed of romantic dinners, soft music, and sweet nothings by the fire. She kissed him again and looked deeply into his steel-grey eyes, feeling their connection growing every minute. The threat of sudden matrimony lingered dangerously in the back of his mind.

"But I don't play any musical instruments," he replied ironically, ignoring the housekeeper's amorous advances. Underneath the constant bullying, crazy housekeeping routine, and toxic cooking, she was strangely attractive—and dangerously persuasive.

"You'll be studying the piano," his mother chimed in. "It's not as difficult as it seems, but I'm sure you're going to fail miserably."

"I'm the editor of the local newspaper. I have no intention of heading the obituaries column—or playing Chopin."

"I don't think anyone has ever died from playing Chopin, but you are advised to be careful."

"Why?" he asked, wondering why he couldn't shut up. His incurable curiosity had gotten him into trouble in the past, and there was nothing he wouldn't do for the sake of a headline.

"You might not have realized it, but Haldon Cottage is a very dangerous place," Hetty replied, sighing as she fluffed his downy pillow. She breathed in a heady blend of manly cologne, stale cigarettes, and well-groomed antagonism. You could learn a lot about a man by fluffing his pillow. She looked forward to learning a lot more. She stroked a restless hand over his cheek and kissed him amorously on the lips. It felt heavenly . . . and left him gasping for air. "And be very careful, my darling, because I don't think I could live without you. Life is so very uncertain and I love you with all my heart. But someone murdered Louise Greene, and who knows what might happen next."

Chapter Four

"That was very good, Neil," Rose Pendlebury sighed, trying not to lose her patience. New music students came in all shapes and sizes . . . and often left her head whirling. As a beginning piano student at the newly formed Haldon Music Academy, Neil Holden had certainly made a name for himself. He paid little attention to Miss Pendlebury's soothing words and hammered randomly at the keys, hoping to make some sense out of this musical nightmare. He had never played the piano in his life, and his efforts were far from melodic. He had no patience and seemed unable to remember even the simplest instruction. It was going to be a very long day.

"Please continue practicing the C Major scale," Rose sighed gracefully. "And mind your fingering, Mr. Holden. It's very important to develop good habits early on. I know it seems unimportant now. You're still just learning the basics, but you'll thank me later. Perhaps Mr. Trent can show you while I make the tea. I'm sure we can all do with a little break."

And with another sigh she hurried from the room, eager to be freed from the contemptuous sounds of Neil Holden's first day at the piano.

"Have you discovered anything?" Lord Hugo whispered. He grabbed a handful of Miss Pendlebury's sheet music and began playing. Lord Hugo was a science professor at the local university, but he was also an incredibly versatile sportsman, criminologist, and a modestly talented pianist. For a few magical moments he played a simple Mozart piano piece with such grace that even Miss Pendlebury drew in her breath. And then he stopped. It was back to crime.

"Well?"

"Well, what, milord?" Neil asked rudely. He was dying for a cigarette and wondered if Mozart smoked. This music gig was going to be the death of him.

"Have you noticed anything relevant for the case?"

"Nothing at all," Neil grunted, and went back to his shocking interpretation of the simple C Major scale. "But if I had to make a guess, I'd say that the wicked nephew committed the crimes."

"Did you arrive at this momentous

conclusion by sifting impartially through the evidence?"

"Not at all," Neil smiled crookedly. "But Alan Pendlebury certainly gains by Louise Greene's death."

Lord Hugo flipped through his notebook and paused before the profile of the notorious nephew. Alan Pendlebury was young, wild, and reckless. As an artist and musician with no intention of settling down, he had made a name for himself in the gossip column. He had spent the last five years touring Europe at his aunt's expense, and played in some of the most disreputable dives. Late nights, stormy romances, and endless debts had cemented his reputation as one of the village's most promising modern villains.

"What do you know?" Lord Hugo asked,

playing the C Major scale with gusto.

"There was a violent argument shortly before the murder," Neil whispered, and stuck his tongue out impulsively. He hated people who did everything perfectly. "Alan Pendlebury is up to his neck in debts and borrowed some of his aunt's money without her knowledge."

"And Louise Greene found out about it?"

"Bravo, milord," Neil smirked. "It's the kind of stuff our newspaper thrives on. The story was featured on page three the day before the crime. And that gives you a motive, if nothing else."

Lord Hugo recalled a recent report about the local troublemaker—and the possible connection it could have to their current crime.

"Something tells me there's more to this story than meets the eye," Lord Hugo added, zipping across the keyboard without a flaw.

"You're not nearly as uninformed as I imagined," Neil laughed contemptuously. "So you won't be entirely surprised to discover that in spite of Alan Pendlebury's rocky relationship with Louise Greene, she left him all her money. And that, in my humble opinion, gave him every reason to commit the crime."

Chapter Five

"What the hell are you doing here?" Alan Pendlebury sneered, making a beeline for the sideboard, where a plentiful supply of brandy promised him an easy way out of life's endless dramas. Between an unsolved murder, an inquisitive aunt, a rocky love life, and no prospects of a steady income, he needed something worthwhile to face the day.

"Your aunt is teaching Neil Holden how to play music," Penny Martin announced in stern tones. She placed the tea tray onto the table and grabbed the brandy decanter from his insipid hands with a finality that signified trouble ahead. His aunt's latest household diva was certainly a handful. After a disastrous bust up over the state of his room, he had hoped to lie low and spend the morning drowning in the comfort of the brandy decanter. Penny Martin had no intention of letting him off lightly . . . and she looked forward to giving him a piece of her mind.

She had taken an immediate dislike to Alan Pendlebury. In spite of his sandy brown hair, boyish good looks, and air of aloof innocence, she was certain that he had committed the crime.

"Good luck," Alan grumbled, and lit a cigarette while her back was turned. He had heard enough of Neil Holden's musical endeavors to last a lifetime. Alan swept a clumsy hand across a photo of Louise Greene on the table before him. It rattled onto the floor with an ominous sense of trouble.

"Poor woman," Penny sighed, and placed the photo back onto the table. She cast Alan Pendlebury a poisonous glance and smiled sweetly. "You were the last person to see her alive."

"And what of it?" he smirked, feeling increasingly unwell. It was coming to something when you couldn't smoke in your own house. Life was certainly complicated, and it was even more so under the vigilant eye of Penny bloody Martin.

"Don't play the innocent, Mr. Pendlebury. You never liked Louise Greene. You quarreled violently shortly before she died, and by the greatest miscarriage of justice, you inherit her money. You should be in prison, not here sponging off your aunt's misplaced generosity."

"I didn't kill her," he screamed

uncontrollably.

"You don't have an alibi for the time of the murder," Penny countered, and poured him a miserable cup of tea.

"As it happens, I do have an alibi," he sputtered anxiously. "Not that it's any of your damned business."

"As an employee at Haldon Cottage, it's my business to ensure that the house runs smoothly," Penny added crisply. "And I don't support crime."

"You're as bad as my aunt," Alan sighed, turning green at the sight of a companionable cup of tea. It was just like his nursery days . . . only they didn't have murders—or Penny Martin. "I was with Anna Henderson."

"And I suppose you were also visiting the vicarage, helping the poor, and aiding the village children's association?"

"Nothing so ambitious," he smiled crookedly.

"Anna Henderson doesn't recall ever seeing you on the day of the murder. This places you in a very delicate position."

"Then I throw myself on the mercy of the court."

"Prison food is quite tasty, Mr. Pendlebury."

"Anna has a selective memory," he gulped uneasily, glancing at today's newspaper, which was opened at the gossip column, where his stormy love life unfolded in full glory. "She wasn't entirely supportive of my relationship with Julia Barton."

"Or Cate Melford, Grace Sanderson, or Alice Jones."

"It's true," he sighed. "But I promised Anna

that I would turn over a new leaf."

"You'll have to do better than that, Mr. Pendlebury."

Penny Martin had met many Alan Pendleburys in her life. None of them had ever committed themselves long enough to make a difference. Of course it was possible that he might eventually settle down, marry a respectable young woman, and have five impossibly troublesome children. But for now, he was trouble with a capital T.

"I dropped in unexpectedly at Anna's cottage. She wouldn't see me, but offered a plentiful supply of advice from the upstairs window."

He paused dreamily, recalling many pleasant romantic interludes spent in the quiet attic room at Anna's cottage . . . until her mother caught them in the act.

"She must have been delighted to read about you in the gossip column," Penny retorted, and flapped the newspaper before him.

"It meant nothing."

How often Penny Martin had heard those very same words, and how often she had wanted to strangle the selfish speaker, whose arrogance and deceit had brought her to the boiling point on more than one occasion. Thankfully, she had married Neville Martin, an utterly dull and respectable solicitor without an ounce of romance, and who had never thought of wandering beyond the garden gate.

"So, what happened?" she asked, ready to wring his neck.

"I ended up having tea with her mother."

He smiled boyishly again and sighed

pathetically. In spite of his complete insensitivity, arrogance, and loose morality, Penny was almost inclined to believe him. He didn't have much to offer the world, but he had a magnetic effect on people and knew how to play them for all it was worth.

"Why did Louise Greene leave you all her money?"

"I have no idea," he sighed spontaneously. His aunt had employed several housekeepers from hell, but Penny Martin certainly took the cake. She was unlike his conception of a modern English housekeeper, he thought, studying her from head to toe. Most housekeepers specialized in frumpy attire, and were awkward, inefficient, and uncomplicated. Penny Martin was dressed to the nines, screamed with astonishing elegance and frightening regularity, and served toxic meals with a graceful hand. And she certainly knew how to ask questions. He shot a quick glance at the Neil Holden and Harold Trent, who were arguing over the cause of Mozart's death. They looked about ready to kill each other, and it was clear that he wasn't going to get any support from either of them.

"Were you having an affair with Louise Greene?" Penny asked briskly.

"No," he stammered weakly. "That is to say— no."

"I don't believe you, Mr. Pendlebury."

"The police didn't, either," he sighed, sinking into his chair. "But I swear there was nothing between us. We used to play music together—that's all. And she was very close to my aunt. I suppose she had no family and decided to take pity on me."

"Or she didn't have time to make a new will," Penny argued compellingly.

She would make a brilliant advocate, Alan thought, feeling increasingly unwell. *And she will certainly send me to the gallows without turning a hair.*

"You'll be delighted to know that we have good news for you," Penny beamed, presenting a compelling case against him. "The police no doubt made a thorough search of the premises after the murder."

"No doubt they did," he sighed, recalling every detail of the nightmare with astonishing clarity. Inspector Meriden had been scrupulous and uncompromising . . . and was quick to assume the worst.

Penny reached into her cardigan pocket and

slapped a single sheet of paper onto the table before him, startling him so much that his teeth rattled uncomfortably.

"What is it?" he asked, shaking from head to toe.

"It's a note from Louise Greene," Penny replied triumphantly.

"Louise never wrote notes—she hated writing and said it was a complete waste of time."

"Then she must have changed her mind. Things like that happen in real life, and they happen when you least expect it. And they can have a fatal effect on your alibi. In this note, Louise Greene expresses her immediate desire to cut you out of her will."

"What are you saying?" he gasped desperately.

"Just what I have been saying all along," Penny added crisply. "That you had every reason to commit the crime."

Chapter Six

"I don't believe him," Elizabeth remarked later at dinner, devouring a hearty meal of roast beef and fluffy mashed potatoes. Dinner at Moriston House was always a treat, and with an unsolved murder case dangling under her very nose, she needed all the help she could get.

"What's that, dear?" Jane asked, and passed her the gravy.

"Alan Pendlebury was lying," she added, licking her fingers gracefully. "I can feel it in my bones."

"He certainly clammed up when I mentioned

Anna Henderson," Penny sighed, buttering a soft bread roll. "But I agree with you, Miss Jones. The case against Alan Pendlebury is watertight."

"Not if Anna Henderson decides to back up his story," Jane replied diplomatically. It was clear that Penny Martin had a personal grudge against their leading suspect, but she preferred to weigh all the facts before arriving at their final destination.

"I can't stand the fellow," Penny grumbled, and poured herself another glass of wine. After a lifetime spent mixing with everyone in London, she knew something about the little intricacies of life.

"I wonder if Anna Henderson really loves him," Elizabeth sighed dramatically. It was difficult when you were eleven years old, and your one ambition in life was to be England's top criminologist. But she wasn't going to give up without a fight.

"You'll soon find out," Lord Hugo smiled, clicking madly at his phone. He hurriedly finished his glass of wine and made a hasty exit onto the terrace.

"Something odd is brewing," Elizabeth gasped, catching her breath. "And I can't help thinking that Alan Pendlebury's relationship with Anna Henderson is at the back of it all."

The appearance of Mrs. Grant always signaled the arrival of something momentous . . . and confirmed her worst suspicions.

"Anna Henderson has arrived. She would like to see you on a matter of the utmost importance."

"Then you had better show her in," Jane smiled playfully. "It's always nice to have a new friend to talk to."

Anna Henderson rushed into the room, colliding with an enormous vase of roses, which she tried to grab before they crashed onto the floor.

"Forgive me for being so clumsy," she gasped, and sank into a chair before she could break anything else. "There are times when I don't know what I'm doing anymore."

"That's quite all right, my dear," Jane replied, and poured her a restorative cup of coffee. "I suppose you have come to tell us that Alan Pendlebury is guilty?"

"How did you know?"

"We are in England, my dear."

"Sorry, I had quite forgotten," Anna sighed, feeling a little better in spite of everything. "And I'm interrupting your dinner, too. I'll come back some other time."

"Stay where you are," Jane replied in a motherly voice. "We're all friends here, and you needn't feel uneasy about anything."

"Do you really mean it?"

Jane studied the young woman with interest, feeling that whatever she had to say simply couldn't wait.

Anna Henderson was a tall and vague young woman of twenty-four, with wavy auburn hair and warm brown eyes. She was pretty in a distant sort of way, with her loose ivory cardigan and unshapely twill skirt. She lived quietly with her mother and worked at the local café. She had led a perfectly quiet life . . . until she met Alan Pendlebury.

Jane Holden's voice was soothingly impassive and wildly accurate in guessing her most private thoughts.

"I suppose your mother didn't approve of Alan."

"She hated him," Anna gushed, unable to stop herself. "And now I can see that she was right."

Jane looked closely at her, sensing the stormy feelings that lived inside her lifeless soul. She saw the gleam of light that flashed into her eyes, the strong heaving of her breast, and the flush that rose to her pale cheeks. She had seen the effects of love's shipwreck before, and knew that they were sailing into stormy waters.

"Before you say anything, I must advise you that your personal feelings are not evidence in a murder case."

Anna stared down at her hands and felt unable to go ahead. She often felt unable to go forward and find her way in an impossible world.

"You probably won't believe it, but Alan did drop in that day."

"Then he might not have committed the crime after all."

"We had a flaming argument," she sighed uncontrollably. "I could have killed him. And then before I knew what had happened, we were in bed together. And before you say anything, you must understand that this is the kind of relationship we have."

Jane listened intently and refrained from offering love advice to their fragile witness. Penny Martin, however, couldn't contain her enthusiasm. It had been some years since she had engaged in anything so stormily romantic, let alone passionate. Her husband, Neville, didn't have the energy to engage in a flaming argument and then make love passionately. He was dismally humdrum, dull, and hopelessly unromantic, and he spent every moment of his wasted life discussing obscure legal cases, following local news, and sleeping at his club. *This was certainly going to be interesting*, she thought, studying the young woman with bold new eyes. *Perhaps she committed the crime and is coming forward with this impossible story to draw suspicion away from herself.*

"Did Alan Pendlebury ever say anything about Louise Greene?" Jane asked gently.

She noted the quick flash of jealousy that lit up in her eyes, and waited for the air to clear.

"We never really talked about anything," she confided reluctantly. "Not anything that mattered, if you know what I mean."

Jane knew precisely what she meant, and hoped for a break in what was turning out to be a perfectly open-and-shut case.

"They had an argument shortly before she died, but then I suppose everyone in the village knows about it."

"Yes, dear," Jane replied mildly. "We live in a time of enhanced communication and exist so transparently that nothing makes any sense until it slaps us in the face."

Anna's mouth dropped to the floor at the incredible clarity of ideas that flowed so freely from the simple village woman who addressed her so confidently.

"I don't know what he really thought about her," she added dreamily. "But Louise was head-over-heels in love with him."

"Did he reciprocate her affection?" Penny asked breathlessly.

"What do you think?" the young woman screamed furiously. "Alan was never faithful, but it's not every day that your former lover turns up dead on your doorstep."

"So they had an affair?"

"He said it meant nothing," she sighed, clenching her teeth furiously. "And I was stupid enough to believe him."

"Are you aware that Louise Greene left him all her money?"

"He won't be getting very much of it if he's convicted of murder."

"Was there anyone else in the house who was there at the time of her death, or who may have had a reason to commit the crime?"

Anna wrinkled her brow severely and came back to herself with the greatest effort.

"There was a visitor," she sighed. "I don't recall her name, but I can't see that she had anything to do with the crime."

"Tell us about her," Jane replied soothingly. "As you say, it probably had nothing to do with the crime, but we'd like to hear your version of the facts."

"Rose Pendlebury's friend dropped in unexpectedly the day before the crime," Anna added absently. "They had studied music together about a hundred years ago. She was an old woman, very dowdy and unassuming. But in spite of her decayed appearance, she played music like an angel. To hear her play the violin was simply breathtaking. I suppose we all have our gifts, no matter how we look on the outside. She had thin grey hair, wore black from head to toe, and looked exactly like a Victorian nanny. She was the kind of woman you couldn't help but forget. But the passion in her eyes was undeniably effective. What *was* her name?" she asked, trying to remember.

If she hadn't wasted every moment of her life in a meaningless love trap with Alan Pendlebury, she might know more about the world around her.

"That's all right, dear," Jane replied sweetly. *Make the client feel comfortable and keep them talking,* she thought, awaiting a glorious outcome.

"Catherine Farringer," Anna blurted out triumphantly. "That was her name—the woman who played the violin so well. It's funny the way that things which you never thought were important suddenly come back to you when you least expect it."

"Yes, my dear," Jane smiled again, closing her notebook with a happy hand. "It certainly is."

Chapter Seven

"So, what do you think about the mysterious violinist?" Elizabeth asked on the following morning, nibbling on a slice of crisp toast.

"I don't know what to think," Penny replied mechanically, serving a decadent portion of eggs, bacon, and fried bread. "But I'll tell you this." She stopped short, spilling coffee onto her new silk blouse. She mopped it up with a monogrammed linen napkin and began shoveling food into her mouth at an alarming pace.

"What?" Elizabeth asked breathlessly. She enjoyed their cozy morning chats over breakfast at

Moriston House. The coffee was fresh, the toast was golden, and the clues were piping hot.

"It probably has nothing to do with the crime."

"She lives nearby," Lord Hugo replied, tossing aside the morning newspaper. He quickly tapped at his mobile phone, answered an endearing text message from his beautiful wife, Lady Rosalin, who was visiting her cousin in London.

"You're up to something, milord," Elizabeth gasped, guessing correctly.

"Nothing that I haven't already been up to before."

"Will Miss Farringer be joining us for tea this afternoon?"

"No, dear," Jane replied, noticing her face drop. "But Rose Pendlebury was so impressed with

Lord Hugo's abilities at the piano, that she has decided to throw a little musical soirée on Friday, and who knows what might happen during the performance at Haldon Cottage."

The following days passed in a frenzy of anticipation and excitement, as Friday dawned bright and clear in the cozy village of Halfereton.

"Do you think there will be another murder?" Elizabeth asked after breakfast, joining her colleagues in the music room at Moriston House. She paused to take in the splendor of the surroundings and the exquisite artwork, and listened as Lord Hugo practiced at the piano with a harmonious hand. *He's quite handsome*, she thought, and sighed as his piece came to a perfect end.

"We've had enough crime for now, Miss

Jones," Lord Hugo replied with a tremendous sigh.

"You look worried, milord," Jane added, guessing his thoughts.

He shot her a quick glance and played brilliantly on the piano, and then he came to an abrupt halt.

"It's not every day that you are invited to play a trio with two professional musicians," he replied, hoping to make it through the day. "And it's not every day that you come face to face with a murderer."

"So you think there will be another crime?"

"I think we should all be extremely careful," he replied mischievously, "and I think I should practice a bit more before Miss Pendlebury realizes that I don't know the first thing about playing the piano."

"Now be very careful, my dear," Jane whispered later that evening at Haldon Cottage. She loved young Elizabeth like a daughter . . . and she knew that there was no stopping her in the pursuit of solving a crime.

"Don't worry," Elizabeth replied, passing a program to Penny Martin, who was blissfully ignorant about classical music.

"Will they be playing *Twinkle, Twinkle Little Star?*" she asked under her breath. "I think I've heard it before, but I can't remember where."

"No, dear," Jane smiled, ushering her to a quiet seat in the back row. "Now remember to keep your eyes and ears open . . . and if you notice anything at all untoward, you know what to do."

"Do I?" Penny asked uncertainly. It wasn't easy being a glamorous middle-aged detective, but she had every hope of solving the crime. Her eyes made a beeline towards lazy Alan Pendlebury, who looked worried and distressed.

"I still think he's guilty," she whispered, noticing the amorous flash in his eyes as Anna Henderson came into the room. It had been some time since a young man had noticed her mere existence, and she felt a pang of envy at the tension of their tangled romance.

"You can decide at the intermission," Jane whispered as the musicians assembled in the elegant music room at Haldon Cottage. It seemed impossible that someone among them was a cold-blooded murderer, and yet it was equally unlikely that the crimes had been committed by an outsider.

"And before you ask, I am now convinced beyond all doubt that Alan Pendlebury is guilty,"

Penny remarked as the musicians took their first bows.

"Do you have any proof?" Jane asked, passing her a bubbly glass of champagne. Penny Martin was elegant, effortless, and outspoken. She always said exactly what was on her mind, and she never apologized when she was wrong. She preferred to let other people take the blame for her own flights of fancy. But she did have a talent for gossip and an unerring tendency to assume the worst. It wasn't a bad perspective, but it could be dismally limiting.

"I saw him," Penny gasped, her diamond earrings dangling dangerously above her glass of champagne. Her husband Neville, who was lost somewhere and mingling with his loyal golf chums, had enjoyed the evening's musical performance immensely. It also gave him a break from having to hear his wife's endless crime reports.

"Yea, dear?" Jane asked patiently.

"I saw Alan Pendlebury sleeping during tonight's performance."

"It doesn't mean that he committed the crime, and there is no court in England that would consider it as evidence."

"A man who can fall asleep during such an amazing recital certainly has something to hide. And did you see the way that Anna Henderson gave him the cold shoulder when he tried to kiss her?" she gushed, gathering strength. "I'm glad she had the good sense to see through his unwelcome amorous advances."

She shot a compulsive glance at Anna Henderson, realizing that she had been completely wrong in her diagnosis of their stormy relationship.

"Do you think so, dear?" Jane asked absently. "I would say that she is as far from being over him as we are from the moon."

Jane Holden was an expert in everything under the sun, and understood the nuances of village romances in a way that often left everyone gasping for air.

"I still think he's guilty," Penny whispered. "But I can understand Anna's feelings."

"I'm sure your insight is much valued," Jane replied, smiling just a little. "Even if it's completely wrong."

"Underneath the rough exterior, he is undeniably handsome," she sighed, changing her mind once again. "No, I'm right—he may have Anna Henderson wrapped around his little finger, but he's not fooling anyone. It's all an act, and tonight he is merely trying to give the impression that nothing ever happened."

"Perhaps he just doesn't like classical music."

Jane Holden was a shrewd observer of life and was also smart enough to know that sometimes the most complicated things turned out to be ridiculously simple.

"He did it on purpose to arouse Anna's attention. And it seems to have worked like a charm. When she arrived, she was confident and vibrant. Now she looks like a shipwreck of nerves, ready to snap at the first moment. Alan Pendlebury knew exactly what he was doing. I've met men like him before. They play the distance ticket, act like you don't exist, and laugh at you when they say they don't love you. And before you even try to contradict it, he's still sleeping at this very minute, which proves that I'm completely right."

"I do think he's overdoing it a bit," Elizabeth whispered, sipping her glass of lemonade. "It's one thing to ignore a beautiful young woman, but he couldn't fail to know that everyone suspects him of committing the crime."

"He knows perfectly well," Penny replied, ready to wring his neck. "And what's more, I think he enjoys it."

They were interrupted by the unwelcome appearance of Jane's son, Neil, who was covering the musical event for the local newspaper. After the sudden collapse of the Arts & Culture correspondent, Neil had found himself at a loss for words . . . and local readership. With a little push and a lot of luck, he had reluctantly agreed to feature the cozy concert at Haldon Cottage. He looked strangely handsome in his vintage tuxedo, and grabbed a glass of champagne from the table with an insensitive hand.

"Can we all go home now?" he asked, fumbling in his pocket for a cigarette.

Jane gently adjusted his bowtie and patted his manly cheek. In some ways, he was still very much a little boy . . . and she wouldn't change him for the world. But she wasn't going to let him off lightly, either.

"What have you found out, dear?"

"Absolutely nothing," he replied, breaking his promise not to smoke at tonight's musical soirée.

Penny Martin gulped uneasily and lowered her voice ominously. As the editor of the local newspaper, Neil Holden was ideally suited to know every detail about village life.

"But you were sitting next to him."

"He snores a lot," Neil replied impulsively. "Probably in C Major."

"Don't be silly," Penny snapped, consulting the program. They had three minutes to solve the crime, and nothing seemed to be working out.

"Have you spoken with the other violinist— what's her name? She played brilliantly, with such lightness and feeling. Anna Henderson was quite right. She plays like an angel, and I can't help feeling that anyone who can play music so beautifully must be off our list of suspects."

"Catherine Farringer gave me the cold shoulder," Neil replied, shrugging it off. He was used to icy responses, threats of violence, and frigid love. As a journalist, he had learned early in his career not to take it seriously. And it gave him a perfect excuse to be an outspoken hypocrite and backstabbing liar.

"Go on," Penny replied cautiously. "I'm almost inclined to believe you."

"She doesn't do interviews and hates journalists."

"Then she's not alone," Penny replied girlishly.

Oddly enough, she liked Neil Holden. She didn't know why, but she admired his uncompromising attitude and standoffish good looks. He was quite the opposite of Jane, and yet they had many things in common. They were both intelligent, inquisitive, and meticulous about details. But he was easier to tease, and she looked forward to celebrating a resounding victory before the end of the musical intermission.

"I did find out something," he replied lazily.

"Don't get too excited, but she doesn't have an alibi. She doesn't have a motive, either, but I know that won't stop everyone from assuming the worst."

"We are in England, dear," his mother chimed in. "And we must examine all the facts before arriving at our destination. But I do agree with you. I don't think she had anything to do with the crime."

Jane glanced at the simple violinist, who looked even more out of place than she had expected. They were interrupted by the momentous appearance of Lord Hugo Anstead, who was compulsively pressing his mobile phone.

"Good evening, milord," Penny said, bowing to their noble partner in crime. "Allow me to congratulate you on a brilliant performance—and a successful conclusion to the case."

"The curtain hasn't fallen yet," he replied breathlessly. "But it may have on Alan Pendlebury."

"So you've found evidence of his guilt?"

"He is unconscious—and someone has tried to poison him."

Chapter Eight

"Poor man," Penny remarked at breakfast on the following morning, her mind whirling. She gulped down a slice of toast with renewed spirit. After a splendid serving of bacon, eggs, and sausages, she felt more like herself again. "I take back everything I said about him. His aunt must be worried sick."

She glanced at the morning newspaper, where the concert of crime unfolded in every gory detail. Neil Holden had been right about everything, but she couldn't help feeling that she was going to have the last laugh.

"Why do you say that?" Penny asked suspiciously.

"You wear your heart on your sleeve," Jane replied, and folded the paper neatly. "I'm just observing that you have a regrettable tendency to change course without warning."

"And what's wrong with that?"

"Nothing that can't be remedied by a good dose of common sense."

"You're hiding something," Penny sighed, sipping her coffee. "And poor Alan Pendlebury is lucky to be alive."

Jane grabbed her crime folder and turned a crisp page, ready to burst Penny Martin's sympathetic bubble.

"Did you know that Alan Pendlebury had a very serious brush with the law? He was accused of attempting to engage in cyber crimes."

"Cyber crimes?" Penny asked anxiously. Her hands trembled as she looked down at her mobile phone and thought about the strange things that happened every day in their perilous modern world.

"Yes, dear," Jane replied thoughtfully. "He befriended lonely old women online, soaked them up with poetical nonsense and sweet loving words, and then he touched them for large sums of money, all the time promising them his undying love and affection. You would be amazed how often people fall headfirst for the trap, and they are getting more and more resourceful . . . and dangerous. They steal private information and make identity theft sound like child's play. They're called romance scammers, and they prey on lonely people, twisting up stories of misfortune while cashing out on people's insecurities. Be very careful when you're online, my dear," Jane continued. "And never share any private financial information with strangers."

"Alan Pendlebury is nothing more than a low-life scumbag," Penny remarked contemptuously, changing her mind again.

"That's more like it, my dear," Jane replied. "He was underage when it happened, but you can see how he still has a way of manipulating people. Anna Henderson is in for a big surprise."

Penny grabbed the newspaper and stared at the story of Alan Pendlebury's poisoning, saying the first thing that came into her mind.

"So, what did the doctors have to say?" Penny asked cautiously. "Or did they prefer to say nothing, and let the press cover any gaps in their diagnosis?"

Elizabeth Branell-Markson stirred from behind the pages of this morning's newspaper and offered a unique point of view.

"Alan Pendlebury's champagne contained soporific medication," she began effortlessly. "Not enough to kill him, but quite enough to ensure that he wasn't going to wake up in time to cause any trouble."

"What do you mean?"

Despite her girlish good looks, beaming smile, and whimsical vintage glasses, Elizabeth Branell-Markson was one of the most well-informed and ruthless journalists in England.

"You're not suggesting that he was quietly hushed up merely to ensure glowing reviews at last night's performance?"

"Someone broke into his room during the

concert."

"I'm not surprised."

A hazy image of Anna Henderson flashed across the canvas of Penny Martin's mind. She tried in vain to remember the details of last night's performance—incredible not merely for the resounding beauty of the music, but for the fact that they hadn't discovered anything new for the case . . . or so she thought.

"Anna Henderson left the music room."

"Yes, dear," Jane smiled triumphantly. "And she refuses to say why Alan Pendlebury's wallet was found in her handbag."

The afternoon passed in a buzz of blurry ideas and half-formed speculations, as the village sleuths awaited the arrival of the talented violinist, Catherine Farringer.

"She's coming," Elizabeth gasped excitedly. "I wonder if she can tell us anything about Alan Pendlebury. As an old family friend and trusted advisor, she might be our ticket to a successful conclusion of the case."

"Don't get your hopes up, dear," Penny smiled, assembling her rambling collection of case notes. "We may find ourselves hosting village tea parties before the day is over."

They smiled as Lord Hugo disappeared through the French windows and rushed down the grand staircase.

"Miss Farringer has arrived, ma'am," Mrs. Grant announced in gilded tones. In some ways, Maggie Grant was a snob, and she prided herself on her meticulous eye for details and ear for village gossip.

"Thank you, Maggie," Jane replied, and poured their guest a fragrant cup of coffee.

Mrs. Grant was known throughout the county for her coffee, which always stirred up something special. She had many secret blends, and roasted them to perfection with astonishing results. Her newest coffee concoction, *Innocence in the Morning,* certainly lived up to its name, and was a robust brew certain to enhance any delicate situation.

"I'm sorry to interrupt you at breakfast," Catherine smiled, sitting down gracefully.

Elizabeth turned a fresh page in her notebook and began to sketch the features of their musical guest. She traced the fragile lines of her weary face and her quietly hollow cheeks, adding a gentle sweep of shadowy interest beneath her still vibrant eyes. Catherine Farringer was not young, pretty, or remarkable, but she had a graceful sense of endurance that added an undeniable interest and beauty to her aging face.

She is very ordinary, Elizabeth thought, capturing the essence of her personality. Perhaps it was this aspect of her character which had allowed her to excel in music.

"I'm afraid I can tell you very little about what happened last night."

"That's quite understandable, dear," Jane said gently. "And on behalf of all of us, may we congratulate you on your performance last night. It was breathtaking. You truly have a unique gift for music."

"Thank you," Catherine smiled, sipping her coffee. "Music has been everything to me. It's my entire life."

"Have you known Rose Pendlebury for very long?"

"Forever," she replied with a gentle smile. "Despite her ladylike appearance and air of modesty, she is a formidable musician. We go back a long time."

"What do you think happened last night?"

Catherine Farringer sighed and tried to recall the blur of dramatic events which had shattered last night's concert at Haldon Cottage.

"I don't know," she replied vaguely. "Rose was naturally very upset about it. I understand there was some kind of robbery upstairs—the police were very vague about it—but I can't understand how it could be connected to Alan's accident."

"So you think it was an accident?" Jane asked

gently.

"What else could it have been?" Catherine replied, opening her eyes widely. "Although I have to say that I was inclined to believe that he staged the whole thing himself . . . and that everything went wrong."

"Why do you say that?" Jane asked gently.

"You must have heard about Alan's past," she continued slowly. "Poor Rose did everything she could to hush it up, but you know what the press is like."

"Yes, dear. I can understand how distressing the whole thing must have been for your friend."

"I suppose he needed money again," Catherine sighed. "Young men can be utterly foolish, and Alan Pendlebury isn't the most scrupulous man in the world."

"Did something happen at Haldon Cottage that could bear any light on our current investigation?" Jane asked patiently. "We're not the police. You may speak in confidence."

"Thank God for that," Catherine replied spiritedly. She sighed again and twisted her hands together. They were the sort of hands that were capable of bringing mere notes of music into breathtaking harmony. They were the sort of hands that never failed to resonate with passion and communicated the world's emotions at the call of her fingertips.

"It just seems strange that Louise Greene would leave all of her money to Alan Pendlebury."

"Yes, it does, dear," Jane replied patiently. "And you think that he was up to his old tricks again?"

"Yes, I do," Catherine replied steadily. "I know it's wicked to say—Rose is a dear friend—but I can't help thinking that Alan Pendlebury murdered Louise Greene."

"Yes, my dear," Jane replied, closing her notebook with a definitive hand. "And I can't help thinking the same thing, too."

Chapter Nine

"What we're lacking in this case is a clear opportunity to have committed the crime," Penny remarked at dinner on the following evening, twirling appetizing strings of savory spaghetti onto a willing fork. It was Italian food night at Moriston House, and Mrs. Grant had prepared an epic feast, with classic spaghetti, crusty ciabatta bread, creamy spumoni gelato, and anise biscotti.

"We're lacking more than that," Lord Hugo replied, finishing his glass of wine. "But it hasn't stopped everyone from assuming the worst."

He glanced at today's newspaper, which

questioned every detail about the Haldon Cottage case.

"What do you think about Catherine Farringer?" Penny asked, licking her fingers gracefully. "She is an amazing musician, but I can't help feeling that she knows more than she was willing to let on."

"She is entirely engaged in her work," Lord Hugo sighed, and poured himself another glass of wine. It was going to be a very long night, and he glanced at a portrait of his wife above the mantel and raised his glass dutifully. "The police have checked everyone's alibis down to the last details, and Catherine Farringer's alibi is watertight."

"I hate watertight alibis," Penny sighed gracefully. "They're usually the first to sink."

"Sink or not, Catherine Farringer was in

London at the time the crime was committed," Lord Hugo replied dismally. "And don't forget, she had no motive to murder Louise Greene."

"I haven't forgotten it," Penny argued. "But I hate loose ends, and that's what we have in this case: nothing but loose ends."

She looked at the bowl of spaghetti and considered another serving, but felt that sometimes you really could have too much of a good thing. Her skirt, which was tightening at an alarming rate, agreed.

The front door sounded in the distance, bringing change and an unexpected visitor.

"I had to see you," Catherine gasped, rushing into the dining room before Mrs. Grant could announce her. It had been nine years since anyone had attempted such an audacious entrance at

Moriston House, and Mrs. Grant resembled a volcano on the brink of a tremendous eruption.

"I must be wrong," Catherine stammered, collapsing onto a chair opposite Lord Hugo Anstead. He was too tongue-tied to say anything and hoped that she would not question why a mere journalist was dining at Moriston House. "But there's simply no other explanation."

Her eyes fixed upon him appealingly, but she realized the truth before he could offer a satisfactory reply.

"Are you here on an interview, Mr. Trent?" she asked politely, her eyes widening. She had always found the press utterly bewildering and hoped to be spared from the scrutiny of endless questions.

"Yes, that's it," he replied, and poured her a sociable glass of wine. *The Halfereton Times* never sleeps."

"Lord Hugo had urgent business in London," Penny replied, crossing her fingers behind her back. "How can we help you?"

Her benevolent blue eyes appealed to Catherine's sense of loyalty and her desire to share exactly what was on her mind. In spite of her ability to interpret complex notes of music and turn them into things of endless beauty, she was unable to recognize the subtle art of manipulation.

"It's about the Haldon Cottage case," she sighed. "I've just remembered something."

How often Penny had heard those words before . . . and how often it had led them down the garden path!

"Please continue, dear," Penny replied, adopting Jane Holden's famous style. Patience and perseverance . . . and give them a shoulder to cry on, and then you might finally hear something worthwhile.

"It's about Alan Pendlebury's poisoning," Catherine replied, and sipped her wine gently. "Everyone has been saying that it was an accident, and I don't wish to say anything against Rose's nephew but . . ."

"Yes, dear?" Penny asked in true Jane Holden style.

"It simply isn't true."

She fidgeted with a napkin on the table and felt uneasy in her mind. It was sometimes difficult to say exactly what was on your mind and at the same time preserve your loyalty.

"I saw him shortly before the concert began. He came into the little area behind the music room.

Harold Trent had gone away for a moment to take a phone call—I remember being worried because I thought he might miss the concert."

Her eyes appealed to his and were met with such sincerity as she had never encountered before.

"Alan came storming into the room and was demanding money from Rose. She told him to pack off—and quite right, too. Oh dear, I feel dreadful to say anything that might look bad for either of them. But everything happened so quickly, and I confess my mind was entirely wrapped up in the performance. I suppose that's why I forgot about it."

"Forgot what, dear?" Penny asked sweetly. She was getting quite good at the whole Jane Holden theme, and looked forward to becoming the next queen of crime. She only hoped that she would be able to hold up the act long enough for Catherine

Farringer to spill the beans.

"It probably has nothing to do with it, but I think you should know."

"Know what?" Penny asked, simmering with impatience. *It wasn't that easy being Jane Holden after all,* she thought, and poured herself another glass of wine to fortify her fraying nerves.

"Alan Pendlebury was drinking," she sighed. "I've spoken to Rose about it, but she doesn't want to face facts. She never does. We were very busy and everything happened so quickly, but I'm convinced that his poisoning wasn't accidental."

"Why is that, dear?"

"I saw him stirring some white powder into his own drink shortly before the performance."

Chapter Ten

"It changes everything," Penny Martin remarked on the following afternoon, assembling her case notes with a light hand. She had been studying Alan Pendlebury's file and lingered over his daredevil photo, trying to recall what it was that had struck her as odd on the evening of his accident.

"I don't agree with you," Elizabeth replied, sipping a cool glass of lemonade. "Alan Pendlebury is an incredible liar, and I don't think that we can assume anything about his accident—if it *was* an accident."

"So you think that he intended to take his

own life?" Jane asked, nibbling on a blueberry scone. "I wouldn't have thought you were so blind about the obvious facts, Miss Jones."

Jane smiled gently and cast her eyes towards this morning's newspaper, where young Elizabeth wrote under the pseudonym of Miranda Jones. Her recent article, *Motives in Crime*, had been the talk of the town.

"On one hand, the case against him is crystal clear," Elizabeth argued passionately. "But if someone wanted to make it look as if he intended to commit suicide, they certainly had the right effect."

"That's more like it, my dear," Jane replied. "Alan Pendlebury is far too arrogant to commit suicide, but we may learn more before the day is out."

Elizabeth sighed and breathed in a deep

measure of healthy country air. There was nothing as beautiful as the English countryside. They had spent a glorious afternoon on the terrace at Moriston House. The sweet smell of garden flowers lingered on her mind, and she could hear the faint trickle of the fountain. Rolling green lawns stretched below, and birds flitted from the hedgerows in a blissful display.

"I don't see how we'll learn anything at all," Penny sighed restlessly. She hated loose ends and false leads. There was only one course of action and she snatched upon it with renewed vigor. She grabbed a blueberry scone and stuffed it into her busy mouth, feeling better for the moment . . . and worse in the long term.

"Cheer up, dear," Jane replied, and poured her another cup of tea. "You'll have plenty of time to decide if Alan Pendlebury is guilty."

"Why do you say that?"

"Because he's joining us for tea on the terrace right now."

Penny observed the arrival of their detestable prime suspect and hurriedly stuffed her case notes into her husband's handy briefcase.

"Alan Pendlebury wishes to see you, ma'am," Mrs. Grant announced coldly. "He is under the impression that he received an invitation to tea at Moriston House."

"Thank you, Maggie," Jane replied graciously. "Show him in."

"You wanted to see me?" Alan asked, dragging his feet. Something about Moriston House made him feel distinctly unwell. Old houses and new money didn't appeal to his outdated sense of justice. Perhaps it was all these women staring at him that made him feel as if he couldn't go on. Or perhaps he just had a lot of growing up to do and was still a spoiled little boy trapped in a man's body.

"How are you feeling today, Mr. Pendlebury?" Jane asked sweetly.

He had never felt so unwell in his wasted life. These three village women were going to be the death of him. It was enough to send him completely over the edge, and he grabbed his flask and gulped a healthy measure of brandy to fortify him for what was coming ahead.

"I'm not dead," he replied, trying to brush it off. He lit a cigarette with shaking hands and puffed on it like a chimney, feeling overwhelmed by their kindness at his misfortune. If there was one thing he had learned in his miserable life, it was never to trust anyone, especially when they asked how you were feeling. He hadn't felt anything in years, and doubted if he would ever feel anything again.

"We just wanted to ask you a few questions about the evening of your accident," Jane smiled, and poured him a medicinal cup of tea. He had hated tea since his nursery days, and watched in horror as Jane added a heaping spoon of sugar and poured in a splash of fresh cream.

"Fire away," he replied, his face contorted in agony.

"Did anything odd happen before the accident?"

"Nothing that hasn't happened before."

Jane studied him for a fleeting moment and felt that for once in his life, he might actually be telling the truth.

"I had an argument with Anna," he sighed

boyishly. "I know what you're going to say. I'm a selfish bastard. We argued all the time. We still argue, but I've never felt that the arguments ever mattered before, and I wanted Anna to know that I was wrong."

"Be careful, Mr. Pendlebury," Jane replied playfully. "That sounds almost like true love."

"Everyone has their faults," he stammered. "I begged Anna to give me another chance."

Jane had heard it all before, but she had not heard it with such conviction. But one thing was certain. She was not going to let Alan Pendlebury pull the wool over her eyes . . . or at least not until he confessed to the crime.

"What happened?"

Alan stared at the tea and did something he never thought he would ever do. He drank it in one quick gulp. And then something unbelievable happened. He actually felt better.

"That woman was staring at me," he babbled strangely. "To be quite honest, it gave me the creeps, and I'm not the type of fellow who faints easily."

"What woman?" Jane asked, and placed her notebook on the table. It was a gesture that she often used to put clients at ease, and it had an immediate effect upon their boyish suspect.

"Cathie Farringer," he replied moodily. "She's my aunt's closest friend, but I can't warm up to her."

"Meaning that she won't give you any money, Mr. Pendlebury?"

"How did you know?"

"We are in England, sir," Jane replied pleasantly. *"The Halfereton Times* was overjoyed to feature every detail of your boyish attempt at cyber crime."

She flapped an old newspaper onto the table and watched as the color drained from his face.

"It was nothing more than a joke," he replied indifferently.

"It's hardly a joke to chat up lonely old women online and then defraud them of their hard-earned savings."

"I didn't know what I was doing," he stammered. "And I needed money. I still need money, but I've gone straight—I swear."

Jane studied him for a fleeting moment, observing all the signs of a habitual liar. His breath came quickly, and there was a dangerous glint in his eyes. His hands twitched and his shoulders slumped. He wasn't the best liar in the world . . . nor was he the worst. He was a very handsome wolf in sheep's clothing, and she wasn't going to let him harm anyone in her immediate flock.

"All right," he sighed vaguely. "I knew exactly what I doing. I never told anyone, not even my solicitor. I was underage at the time, and in all honesty, I don't even regret what I did. It was quite fun, actually. I used to get a kick out of it. For the first time in my life, I had a job. I had a purpose. I was a consultant, an advisor, a lover, and a best friend. I was a kind of cyber gigolo, and I gave them nothing but pleasure. I received six proposals of marriage and one offer for adoption. You would be amazed at how credulous some people are. They would believe anything. At one point, I had ten old ladies wrapped around my fingers. God, it used to make me laugh."

"Then you certainly have some explaining to do."

"I did my time," he sighed innocently. "And I paid them all back."

"Your aunt paid them all back, Mr. Pendlebury," Jane argued. "And it may explain why you murdered Louise Greene."

"I didn't kill her."

"I have always found it odd that a woman you claim to have hardly known would leave you her entire fortune, although you may find it difficult to cash in if you are convicted of murder. You had every reason to commit the crime."

"All right," he admitted reluctantly. "I had her going, but this time it was . . . more intimate."

"Leave the room, Miss Jones," Jane advised, nodding at young Elizabeth. It was not the sort of conversation to be heard by young ears. "And call the police on your way."

Alan Pendlebury didn't care who heard what he had to say. His solicitors had been dead set on a school-boy menu of silence, caution, and distance. But the time had come to settle the score.

"I didn't commit the crime."

"You have a remarkable talent for deception, Mr. Pendlebury. And before you go any further, tell me one thing. Why did you play up to Louise Greene? Was it sufficiently thrilling to make love to a lonely middle-aged woman? Or was she merely an easy conquest? Men like you have an absurd perception of vanity. Or was it like everything else in your life, merely another business transaction?"

Alan shifted in his chair and lit another cigarette. He hated endless cups of tea, pointless questions, and inquisitive private detectives. But if he could clear his name, he might find life a little more worth living.

"You probably won't believe it, but I did care for her."

"Try again, Mr. Pendlebury."

"It wasn't love with a capital L, but we had some good times together. We could tell each other everything and never worry about what anyone might say. There is something about an older woman—I don't know quite how to explain it—but all the petty crap you deal with on a daily basis with young women flies out the window. There are no meaningless arguments or jealousies. You can just move on and know that at the end of the day, someone is always there for you."

"And you inherit all of Louise Greene's

money now that she is dead."

"I didn't know about it."

Jane drummed her slender fingers on the table and stopped with an abruptness that left him feeling that the worst was yet to come.

"All right, I *did* know it—but I didn't believe it for a moment."

"And your fainthearted attempt at honesty gives you every reason to have committed the crime."

Chapter Eleven

"I always knew he was a low-life scumbag," Penny remarked on the following morning, indulging in a gooey cinnamon bun. She licked a dangerously sweet blob of icing from her finger and considered the case from a new perspective.

"What's that, dear?" Jane asked, and poured her another cup of coffee.

"I should have trusted you from the beginning. Alan Pendlebury had every reason to commit the crime."

"Not *every* reason," Jane argued, smiling from behind the pages of this morning's ludicrous newspaper. Weather, politics, gossip, and sports seemed unreal after their interview with Alan Pendlebury . . . and their unsolved crime.

"Where is Lord Hugo?" Elizabeth asked suspiciously, hearing the ominous sound of the clock in the clock. There was something about eight o'clock that always rattled her. It was a defining moment of the day, and she couldn't help feeling that something momentous was working its way into the headlines of life. It was a perfect morning in every way. The weather was fair, and a gentle breeze floated past the French windows, bringing the softness of wildflowers and dewy grass. She could hear the faint sound of the fountain trickling below the terrace, and birdsong echoed cheerfully in the distance . . . until Mrs. Grant stormed into the room.

"Sorry to disturb you, ma'am," Mrs. Grant announced grandly. "Anna Henderson wishes to see you. She says it's a matter of life and death."

"That's quite all right, Maggie," Jane replied. "Show her in—and we'll need another pot of coffee, please. On second thought, better make it two."

"I'm sorry to bother you at breakfast, but something dreadful has happened."

"Yes, dear?" Jane asked gently.

"I didn't want to notify the police."

How many times Jane had heard those very words . . . and how many times it had been a complete waste of time. But something in the manner and tone of Anna's voice told her that there was more to this story than meets the eye.

Anna rummaged the depths of her floppy tote bag and presented a surprisingly large parcel of even greater interest. The Royal Mail never let you down.

"We received it yesterday. As I said, I didn't want to go to the police. I thought you might be able to help me."

Jane opened the parcel and found an ordinary blackmail letter. It was the kind of thing that happened every day in England. Blah, blah, blah, she had heard it all before. Someone was threatening to expose Anna Henderson for certain photos she had taken while under Alan Pendlebury's toxic love spell. A couple of insanely blurry images added zing to an otherwise flat prospective. Some people had no imagination and nothing better to do than to try their luck on the other side of the law. The only thing that was unusual about it was the fact that they had even tried at all. And the size of the parcel was strangely curious. It seemed very large for such a small demand. £100 was hardly worth the postage, let alone the prospect of an official inquiry. Perhaps this was merely a first attempt, just to see which way the wind was blowing. And then, bang! Here comes something more interesting: £50,000 for silence—and a false promise to disappear quietly into the woodwork. Everyone in the village knew about Anna's stormy relationship with Alan Pendlebury. The *Halfereton Times* was hopelessly romantic. Why attempt a rather feeble dose of blackmail on a young woman without many prospects and even less ready cash?

"I can't believe it," Anna sighed, burying her face in her hands. "But I'll tell you one thing. Alan might be a backhanded liar and womanizer. He might even be a cold-blooded murderer, for all I know. But blackmail is not his cup of tea."

"Are you absolutely certain?"

Somehow the simplicity of the suggestion took her completely off guard. Jane had a magical way of getting to the heart of the matter . . . and she knew exactly how to keep her talking.

"I know what you're thinking, but Alan is far too complacent to ever go in for anything that doesn't offer immediate rewards. He lives for the moment, and is one of the most selfish people I have ever met in my life."

"Selfish people are quite capable of blackmail, my dear," Jane replied easily. "In fact, they specialize in it. And they are also capable of committing murder."

Anna shifted uneasily and twisted her hands in a reckless manner. She clenched her hands so strongly that her veins wiggled beneath her thin skin. Something very strange was working its way into the conversation, and Jane was determined to find out exactly what it was.

Jane studied her for a fleeting moment, sensing again that look of agony which had been spreading like wildfire across her face. But there was something else. She seemed to be on the brink of something important when she stood up and began tottering like a tree. Her breath came quickly, until she began gasping uncontrollably. And then she crashed onto the floor in a finality that seemed horrifyingly unreal.

"Call an ambulance at once—although I'm afraid it may be too late."

Penny Martin grabbed her phone and alerted the authorities about the dangerous situation that had developed at Moriston House.

Jane hurriedly attended the lifeless young woman, but she was going to need more than mere a girl-scout revival. Jane made a cursory examination of the area and quickly rummaged through the young woman's handbag. She tossed aside old keys, a couple of weary banknotes, and a wallet full of unnecessary photos of her wasted life with Alan Pendlebury. Some of the photos were stupidly risqué, and showed floppy body parts that were better left out of the limelight. It all seemed so out of place in her otherwise boring life. Why were people careless enough to photograph their most intimate moments? It was nothing that Jane hadn't seen before, but it was certainly enough to cause trouble.

And then she came across something that finally made sense. There was a note, penned in a sloppy and boyish hand, which threatened to send some the photos to the newspaper . . . unless a handsome donation was duly paid. Alan Pendlebury had wasted no time. But there was something else.

Jane grabbed a small bottle of useless diet pills and unscrewed the lid. So-called health claims and promises of quick weight loss had lured many gullible people to stuff themselves with obscure laboratory herbs and unnecessary chemicals. Anna Henderson didn't strike her as the type of person to indulge in fads, but she recalled a moment during their interview when the young woman fumbled in her purse and popped something into her mouth. But there was something else. A brief note from Alan, saying *'hope it helps,'* had been attached to the bottle.

Jane unscrewed the lid and made a

cautionary examination of the contents.

"Everything happened so quickly," Penny breathed heavily. "I only hope she didn't try to take her own life. I know she's been having a difficult time at home, and she seemed so desperate, as if nothing mattered any more. Oh God, is she dead?"

"No, dear, but she needs medical attention immediately."

The sound of the ambulance rambling along the private drive brought a conflicting sense of relief and urgency to the dire situation.

"Give me one of those," Penny remarked, grabbing the bottle. "I daresay I could lose a pound or two."

She passed an elegant hand over her puffy waist and sighed at the regrettable state of her figure. She seldom said no to a slice of Mrs. Grant's decadent chocolate cake, and she was often love struck at the sight of buttery pastries, homemade tarts, and gooey puddings.

But Jane's voice of reason once again brought her gourmet dreams to a crashing halt.

"Don't take it!"

"Why?"

"Because someone has laced these pills with poison."

Penny recoiled at the horror of it all and said the first thing that came into her mind.

"It's dreadful—I might have died."

Jane had a quick word with the medical attendants and grabbed her impetuous colleague by the hand, leading them out into the privacy of the hall.

"Will she be all right?" Penny shivered

anxiously. She peeked into the elegant room, where she saw the medical attendants working furiously to revive the unfortunate victim. They appeared to be making some progress, and she watched as they busily wheeled her to the ambulance. A moment later they were tearing down the gravel drive en route to the hospital.

The full horror of the situation had finally dawned upon her, but she couldn't help feeling that the worst was yet to come.

"Why would Alan Pendlebury want to harm her, let alone murder her?"

Penny shivered again and felt that something important hadn't come to light. The case against Alan, which had always been feeble and improbable, had grown into something more worthy of his detestable personality.

"Well, what do you think?" Penny asked furiously. "Did Alan Pendlebury attempt to murder his girlfriend?"

She recalled his contemptible attitude and the subtle but provokingly effective way that he never seemed to commit himself. He was a hopeless cheater, a brazen liar, and a daring womanizer. He was also a convicted romance scammer, and understood the subtly invidious methods of gaining trust and confidence from his innocent victims. On the surface, he was ideally placed to have committed the crime. Perhaps Anna had threatened to expose him. Or better yet, perhaps she had given him a dose of his own medicine and had blackmailed him into silence. But the result had taken her by surprise.

Penny stared at Jane Holden, wondering what was going on in her industrious mind.

It was all very fine and grand to be England's most celebrated detective—the teatime treats were diabolically decadent—but at times Jane Holden's professional reticence was intolerable.

Penny sighed as she heard the sound of the ambulance fading in the distance. The case—a matter of life and death—was out of their hands now.

"Poor Anna—I hope she'll be all right. Her mother will be devastated when she hears the news."

Mrs. Henderson was a quiet and respectable middle-aged woman, who worked incessantly to make ends meet. Her daughter's involvement with a known criminal had already given her an unpleasant taste in her mouth.

Jane had just finished a brief conversation with Mrs. Henderson, who was overcome with panic and grief at the news of her daughter's poisoning.

She clicked off her phone and stared out into the garden, where life wandered at a leisurely pace and crime didn't dare to show its ugly hand. The sound of her voice came as a total surprise.

"For once I totally agree with you."

"You do?" Penny asked, unable to believe her ears. Jane was one of the smartest people she had ever met, but she was also one of the most stubborn.

"Yes, dear," Jane replied, admiring the wisteria trellis. There among twisted vines and leafy secrets, some of the most beautiful things had bloomed. Their case was exactly the same though not quite as beautiful.

"You've said it from the beginning, and your instinct is never wrong. You may at times take a wrong turn and arrive at an unknown destination, or may even go off the charts and disappear into thin air. But one thing is certain. There is no doubt that Alan Pendlebury had every reason to commit the crimes."

Chapter Twelve

"Who do you think committed the crimes?" Elizabeth Branell-Markson asked on the following day at lunch, nibbling on a savory ham sandwich.

"I don't know, dear," Penny replied, and sighed as she inhaled everything in sight. "I don't know anything anymore."

"Don't despair," Elizabeth replied, tossing a piece of the sandwich to Lord Hugo's faithful dog, Butterfield, a wiry Fox Terrier with a keen sense of justice. "Sorry, I was asking Butterfield what he thinks about the case. He's met plenty of criminals in his life."

"He probably knows offhand who murdered Louise Greene," Penny sighed again. "Give him another sandwich, dear. At this stage, we need all the help we can get."

"Have you seen this morning's news?" Lord Hugo asked, and poured her another glass of lemonade.

"Everyone in the world reads the *Times*," Penny moaned. "And they've squeezed every drop out of this case. I don't think we'll ever solve the case . . . or know the truth."

"It's not as complicated as you imagine."

"Thanks for your vote of confidence, milord, but this time I must confess that nothing makes sense."

Penny stuffed another sandwich into her busy mouth and glanced at today's glorious news.

A Little Bird Told Me

By Miss Emilia Manners, Social Correspondent.

A little bird forecasts danger at Haldon Cottage, where life is certainly no bed of roses. A stranger was observed near the crime scene after the attempted poisoning of Anna Henderson, who is expected to make a full recovery. The police investigation indicates that A. P.'s alibi isn't nearly as watertight as initially suspected. Is there cause for speculation? If so, it wouldn't be the first time, my dears. Has passion overtaken reason? Join us for a cup of tea and we will see what happens underneath the rose arbor . . .

"Your column is so inspiring," Penny remarked, swelling with pride. Jane Holden's pen was the secret weapon behind the popular column, and she dished out dirt with uncompromising style and grace. Her wit and wisdom had saved the day on more than one occasion, and the newspaper's instinct was never wrong.

"Thank you, dear, but we're not out of hot water yet."

"So there might be another murder?"

Penny shivered at the thought of another crime in their quiet English village. And she shivered again, knowing that Jane Holden was always right.

"Rest assured, there is a light at the end of this tunnel."

"Then you know who committed the crimes?"

"In one of Lord Hugo's dubious moments as an inspiring pianist and ruthless undercover agent for the Mayfair Detective Agency, he has uncovered something unusual for the case."

"Ring up the suspects, Miss Jones," Lord Hugo announced, setting the ball in motion.

"What am I supposed to tell them?" Elizabeth gasped, spilling her glass of lemonade. She parodied her role as the perfect secretary, and her voice oozed with compulsive persuasiveness and catchy charm.

"Good afternoon, sweetie, sorry to bother you, but you're invited to dinner at Moriston House on Friday. Oh, and by the way, you're our prime suspect, so remember to smile when you're arrested for murder."

"Something like that, Miss Jones," Lord

Hugo replied, flashing a devilish smile. "I knew we could rely on you. You always think of everything."

Chapter Thirteen

"They're here!" Elizabeth Branell-Markson dashed down the great hall at Moriston House, eager to solve the case. She skipped past Lord Hugo Anstead's glorious collection of artwork, and narrowly escaped knocking over one of Mrs. Grant's breathtaking floral arrangements. She had spent a sleepless night checking alibis, devouring case notes, and examining potential motives. Nearly everyone had a motive in the case, but she still couldn't understand the reason for Louise Greene's death.

"I know what you're thinking, dear," Penny called, huffing and puffing as she attempted to outpace the nimble young detective. "But I think we're in for a major surprise."

"Are we late?" Anna Henderson gulped, looking modestly elegant in a simple black frock with a boxy hemline. "I hope you don't mind, but I brought my Mum along. She's been following every detail of the Haldon Cottage case in the newspaper."

"Welcome to Moriston House," Elizabeth replied grandly, and ushered them into the elegant sitting room. Moriston House sparkled on the occasion of the unveiling of a crime, and tonight was no exception. The house had been featured in every magazine in England for its luxurious traditional décor, historical significance, and captivating gardens. But it was on such nights when its beauty truly came into focus.

"Any chance of a cocktail?" Alan Pendlebury

asked, dragging his feet.

"You mustn't say such things," his aunt whispered indulgently. She glanced at her nephew and wondered if he would ever truly grow up. Something in the back of her mind told her that he had a very long way to go before he became a responsible and trustworthy man. Perhaps it would never happen, or worse still, perhaps he really had murdered Louise Greene. No, it was impossible, she thought, sipping a sparkling glass of champagne.

"Is it true that the case is solved?" Catherine Farringer asked, joining them.

"God knows," Alan smirked, pouring a lethal amount of whisky into his glass. "But one thing is certain. We're not here tonight to view the art." He raised his glass towards an elegant painting of their debonair host, Lord Hugo Anstead, who had yet to make an appearance. "That chap looks vaguely familiar, and no, my dear aunt, I'm not drunk yet, but I hope to be before the night is out."

He stared at the towering piece of art and raised his glass again.

"Handsome chap—can't place where I've seen him, but it's damned decent of him to fortify us so generously. Cheers, milord—here's to crime."

"Cheers," Lord Hugo replied amiably, joining the party. "And now you can tell us why you committed the crime."

Chapter Fourteen

"You've got to be joking," Alan replied, lighting a cheap cigarette. He puffed little circles into the air and caught an unexpected glance at Anna, who specialized in giving him a contemptuous reply. "Why would I want to murder Louise Greene?"

It was moments like this when he wondered why he couldn't remain silent. His lawyers had advised him to say nothing. Why could he never follow even the simplest advice? Why must he always stir up trouble? And why could he never leave well enough alone?

"We've said it all along," Jane Holden replied, sipping a sparkling glass of champagne. "You conducted an illicit and manipulative relationship with the housekeeper, Louise Greene. You toyed with her affections just long enough for her to leave her entire fortune to you, and then when the moment was right, you murdered her, knowing that no one would ever find out the truth."

"Village gossip," he replied acidly. "It's all lies and malicious village gossip."

"Never underestimate the power of local opinion, Mr. Pendlebury. It explains nearly everything, but it doesn't explain why you're heartless enough to deny that you killed her."

"I didn't murder her!"

"You also have a prior conviction for romance scamming," Jane replied easily. "It is a very serious form of cyber crime, and sadly, it is growing at a phenomenal rate among ruthless individuals who would do anything for money. Although you were underage at the time, you used social media to befriend lonely and vulnerable women, and you showered them with endless sweet nothings and promises of undying affection. Then when you had them safely wrapped around your little finger, you touched them for large amounts of money, and left them to carry the can."

"It was a joke, that's all," he stammered hopelessly.

"Theft is no joke, Mr. Pendlebury," Jane replied briskly. "And neither is murder."

"They got their damned money back," he grunted sourly. "Louise Greene knew exactly what she was doing. She had no relatives and had saved every penny that she earned since she was a girl. It was stupid of her to tell me—she knew about my past, but she was delighted to overlook everything."

He smiled weakly and shuddered at the way things were going. If he wasn't careful, he might find himself arrested before the night was out.

"How sweet of you," Jane replied ironically. "And though everyone knows you didn't care two figs about her, you will be happy to know that you weren't the only one who had a reason to commit the crime."

Chapter Fifteen

"There's something that's been bothering me all along," Penny Martin complained, nibbling on a savory cheese canapé. She loved these evenings of crime at Moriston House—the food was phenomenal—but several questions lingered painfully in the back of her mind. The things that bothered her on a daily base were often horrifyingly numerous and utterly absurd. She wrinkled her eyebrows and plunged into the latest iniquity with a fearless approach.

"What was that strange business early in the case about the dream? And how is it connected to the legend about poor Emma Haldon and her dog?"

She leafed through her fabulous collection of case notes and paused over Rose Pendlebury's sensational initial statement. The famous violinist had come to them in a state of considerable distress, and until this moment, they had been unable to identify the source of that misery. She glanced at a vintage photo of Emma Green and her faithful Collie. *How was that tragedy connected to their present case?* At the time, Penny Martin had been living a glamorous life in London. She splurged endlessly at luxury boutiques. Her evenings were spent entertaining friends in their fashionable flat in Mayfair or enjoying the spectacular dining experiences of a cultured London socialite. She cast a hopeful eye at Jane Holden's captivating poem that had been dedicated to her poor deceased friend.

Cottage Dreams

In memory of Emma Haldon

By Miss Emilia Manners, Social Correspondent.

There's a little cottage that I know
Where blushing roses always grow
Behind the woods and near the stream
Where idle thoughts are known to dream
Where bluebells wander o'er the knoll
And primrose carpets fill your soul
Where birdsong floats on painted skies
And days and nights drift idly by
Where drowsy dreams wander far
And sleepy clouds hide silver stars
Where life's sweet songs serenade
And cheer and laughter never fade.

"Jane, I'm simply going to die if you don't tell me," Penny gushed anxiously.

"Tell you what, dear?"

"How is the unfortunate legend of Emma Haldon connected with our present tragedy?"

"Sadly, it was used as so many things are nowadays, as a bait to conceal the truth about the murders."

"So Emma Haldon was murdered after all?"

Penny shivered at the thought of that poor village woman and her faithful dog. Until now, the mystery had never been solved. Something told her that the worst was yet to come.

"The remains were discovered in the garden at Haldon Cottage yesterday."

"Oh my God—and you think that someone here murdered her?"

"Yes, dear," Jane replied, turning her attention to Anna Henderson's mother, Grace, who had been silent until now.

Grace recalled the strange phone call she had received from Miranda Jones, and wondered why anyone would want to invite them to dine at Moriston House.

Grace Henderson was a tired and ordinary middle-aged woman, with wispy grey hair and an unnoticeable personality. For as long as she could remember, she had struggled to make ends meet. Since her husband's death, she had looked after their only daughter, Anna. She wore a shapeless black vintage dress and floppy old shoes. Her old wedding ring fit uncomfortably on her stiff finger. All of her other jewelry had been sold. But beneath her faded brown eyes a deadly secret had remained untouched until now.

"You're not seriously suggesting that I murdered Emma Haldon?" she asked indifferently.

But Jane wasn't finished yet.

"And when Louise Greene discovered the truth, you murdered her, too."

Chapter Sixteen

"How did you ever discover the truth?" Penny asked on the following morning, admiring their inspiring photo in the morning newspaper. The *Halfereton Times* had been glowing in their praise, and had left not a stone unturned.

"It was a process of elimination, dear," Jane replied patiently. "Rose Pendlebury had no motive in the case, and was truly frightened. Someone was trying to intimidate her, and it seemed strange for someone so entirely unconnected to village life. As a professional violinist and newcomer, it seemed unlikely that she had any connection to the crimes. I knew at once that she was telling the truth."

"I was convinced that Alan Pendlebury was guilty."

"Yes, dear," Jane replied, and poured her another cup of tea. "That's because you had the misfortune to feel sorry for the Hendersons."

Penny shivered as she recalled Grace Henderson's dramatic arrest . . . and her daughter's complete breakdown. It certainly wasn't easy being part of England's savviest private detective agency, but moments like this made it all worthwhile.

"Why did Grace Henderson murder Emma Haldon and Louise Greene?" Elizabeth asked, eating everything in sight. She grabbed the last slice of bacon and smiled as Penny Martin's hopeful mouth salivated in jealousy.

"It's quite simple, my dear," Jane replied. "It

wasn't simple at the time, but thanks to Lord Hugo's undercover investigation, we discovered something rather spectacular."

"And?"

"He found out that no one had a true motive to commit the crimes."

"How is that?"

"Look at it this way, Miss Jones. Rose Pendlebury has spent her entire life devoted to music. She wasn't living in the village at the time of Emma Haldon's mysterious disappearance. What possible reason would she have in the case? None at all. The same applies to Catherine Farringer. She is equally devoted to music and a loyal family friend. Neither of them ever knew Emma Haldon. Alan Pendlebury is a complete idiot and far too lazy to engage in murder. Yes, I know what you're thinking.

As a convicted romance scammer, he came perilously close to the edge, but as much as I detest the man, I had to face facts. He didn't murder anyone."

"What about Anna Henderson?" Elizabeth asked, licking her fingers gracefully.

"That's where things became complicated," Lord Hugo replied, tossing aside this morning's newspaper. He smiled as he caught sight of a photo of Neil Holden, looking embarrassingly boyish as Rose Pendlebury's brightest new pupil. He was never going to let him live this down—or escape punishment for hitting the wrong notes.

"Only someone closely connected with Anna Henderson could have tampered with her diet pills. Now, Alan Pendlebury is one of the most selfish men in England, and it seemed unlikely that he would have taken the time to write a note to his beloved Anna, let alone poison her. His entire life is wrapped up in himself—and gaining the affection of wealthy women. He succeeded in wrapping Louise Greene around his little finger. He had no reason to do anything but wait. And the more he waited the more money he would get. And then we stumbled upon something interesting: the sudden death of Anna Henderson's father, Roger. No one ever questioned his death. He drank excessively, and one evening, he had fallen down the stairs and never regained consciousness. That was the end of Roger Henderson. But what if his death *wasn't* an accident?"

"You're not suggesting that Grace Henderson murdered her husband?"

"Yes, dear," Jane replied gently. "And it was for this reason that she murdered Emma Haldon.

She had discovered the truth and intended to go to the police. Grace Henderson silenced her before this could happen, and when Louise Greene discovered the truth, she murdered her in cold blood."

"How dreadful," Penny shivered uncontrollably. "But are you seriously suggesting that Grace Henderson poisoned her own daughter?"

"Yes, dear," Jane replied thoughtfully. "She would have done anything to conceal her secret . . . and she wouldn't have turned a hair if her daughter would have died."

They were interrupted by the appearance of Mrs. Grant, who shuffled into the elegant room with an additional tray of provisions . . . and the latest news.

"Good morning, milord," she announced with dignity.

"Good morning, Maggie. Lady Rosalin is due to return home today. Has a parcel from London arrived?" He smiled as he recalled the lovely earrings he had purchased for his wife, and he looked forward more than anything to holding her in his arms.

"Yes, milord. Butterfield nearly tore the fellow to pieces. The Royal Mail makes him exceedingly uneasy. I placed the item on your desk. And may I offer my congratulations on the successful conclusion of the Haldon case."

They were interrupted by the sound of the old phone in the hall, which clattered desperately.

Mrs. Grant hurried into the hall and answered the restless noisemaker. She returned a moment later, beaming with pride.

"That was Neil Holden, milord. He said

quite clearly that you are a dead man. I assume it's about that delightful photo in this morning's newspaper. Personally, I thought he looked so sweet and innocent, just like a little boy. No one would ever guess how horrible he really is. Oh, and by the way, milord, there was something else. Everyone is talking about it. There has been another murder in the village. . ."

Jennifer Anne Girardin
Author & Classical Pianist

Greetings from Moriston House Mysteries!
I'm originally from San Francisco, California, and I'm
currently residing in Historic Ridgewood in Canton,
Ohio. In addition to writing Moriston House British
mysteries, I am also a classical pianist and music
historian at Andante Piano Studio. I am passionate
about the creative process and also enjoy opera, art,
history, gardening, nature, cooking, photography,
architecture, and design. When I'm not lingering over
my antique piano and playing endless classical sonatas,
I'm enjoying quality time with my loving friends and
family. Happy reading from Moriston House books!

Contact Moriston House Mysteries

Join Jennifer Anne Girardin and Moriston House books online for the latest author news, photos, insights, books, art, exploration of classical music, gardening, and lots of laughter!

Email: jenniferannegirardin@gmail.com

Andante Piano Studio in Historic Ridgewood Canton, Ohio. andantepianomusicstudio.com

Instagram:
https://www.instagram.com/moristonhousebooks/

Threads:
https://www.threads.net/@moristonhousebooks

Facebook:
https://www.facebook.com/moristonhousebooks/

X: https://twitter.com/moristonhouse

Pinterest:
https://www.pinterest.com/moristonhouse/

Drop in for tea and mystery at:
https://moristonhouse.wixsite.com/my-site

Andante Piano Studio

Historic Ridgewood Canton, Ohio

Acknowledgments

Cover image: File: William Henry Margetson 006 (24533642487).jpg courtesy of Wikimedia Commons public domain.
Margetsonhttps://commons.wikimedia.org/wiki/File:William_Henry_Margetson_006_(24533642487).jpg

Cuckoo Line Art Bird Image courtesy of GDJ, Pixabay.
https://pixabay.com/vectors/cuckoo-animal-line-art-bird-5310825/
https://pixabay.com/service/license/

Frame Flourish courtesy of GDJ, Pixabay.
https://pixabay.com/vectors/frame-divider-flourish-ornamental-5818661/
https://pixabay.com/service/license/

Altered image of Petersfield Cottage Hospital. Wellcome L0001358.jpg. Courtesy of Wikimedia Commons and Wellcome Images.
https://commons.wikimedia.org/wiki/File:Petersfield_Cottage_Hospital._Wellcome_L0001358.jpg
https://creativecommons.org/licenses/by/4.0/deed.en
https://wellcomeimages.org/indexplus/obf_images/ab/ab/a8f42
9e7712950d1c1820e29f4c0.jpg
http://catalogue.wellcomelibrary.org/record=b1286940

Acknowledgments

The Village Homes of England by Sydney R. Jones courtesy of Pen, Flickr.
https://www.flickr.com/photos/revivaling/5557840351/
https://creativecommons.org/licenses/by-sa/2.0/

Altered image of East Budleigh Devon UK courtesy of vinsky2002, Pixabay. https://pixabay.com/service/license/
https://pixabay.com/illustrations/east-budleigh-devon-uk-vintage-old-4288376/

Altered image of Vintage Ladies Tea Jacket, courtesy of The Old Design Shop. https://olddesignshop.com/2015/10/vintage-ladies-tea-jacket/

Image of Japanese Rose Flowering Branch Clip Art courtesy of The Old Design Shop.
https://olddesignshop.com/2014/07/japanese-rose-flowering-branch-free-clip-art/

Typewriter image courtesy of Wikimedia Commons.
http://commons.wikimedia.org/wiki/File:Skrifmaskin,_Underwood-maskin,_Nordisk_familjebok.png

Teapot image courtesy of The Old Design Shop.
http://olddesignshop.com

Moriston House Mysteries

Sweet Nothings

Coming soon

Made in the USA
Monee, IL
15 August 2024